Slumber Party Funbook

Editorial Director: Marge Kennedy

little monks on the wisdom tree

Planning Your Party

Gwen is planning to have a slumber party at her house. For her first step, she made a planning checklist. You can make party plans just like Gwen!

My Party

TWO WEEKS BEFORE PARTY:

√ Get permission from my parents.
√ Make a guest list.
√ Pick a day and time.
√ Send out invitations.

ONE WEEK BEFORE PARTY:

√ Confirm guest list.
√ Plan my menu.
√ Start collecting things I'll need for games and other activities.
√ Prepare party favours.

ONE DAY BEFORE PARTY:

√ Buy food.
√ Clean party room.
√ Wash bedding that guests will use.
√ Double check that I've got the things I need.

DAY OF PARTY:

√ Prepare snacks.
√ Relax and enjoy!

INVITATIONS: Now you're ready to invite your guests! You can make photocopies of the invitations on pages 3 and 4 or better still draw, colour and create your own cards. Then fill them in and send them out!

Gwen
Come to My Party!
INVITATION

Gwen
I'm Having a Party!
Invitation

Gwen
It's a Party!
Invitation

Given by: ______________________

Phone Number: ______________________

When: ______________________

Where: ______________________

Reason for My Party: ______________________

Given by: ______________________

Phone Number: ______________________

When: ______________________

Where: ______________________

Reason for My Party: ______________________

Given by: ______________________

Phone Number: ______________________

When: ______________________

Where: ______________________

Reason for My Party: ______________________

Guest List

Gwen is inviting girls from her class to her party. She wants to draw a picture of each one for her scrapbook. You can draw pictures of your friends for your own collection.

My friend ________

My friend ________

My friend ________

My friend ________

My friend ________

My friend ________

Menu Planner

Gwen wants to be sure to have something to eat that each girl will especially like. She prepared a survey to get her guests' opinions about her menu. You can make a survey, too—or you can use Gwen's questionnaire.

Food Survey

DINNER FOOD

Do you like pizza? ___ YES ___ NO
What's your favourite topping? ______________________
What pizza topping don't you like? ______________________

SNACK FOOD

Which snacks do you like or dislike?

	LIKE	DON'T LIKE
Doughnut	___	___
Popcorn	___	___
Fries	___	___
Samosa	___	___
Other: ______________	___	___

DRINKS

Which drinks do you like or dislike?

	LIKE	DON'T LIKE
Milk	___	___
Fruit Juice	___	___
Water	___	___
Iced Tea	___	___
Other: ______________	___	___

ICE CREAM

What's your favorite flavour? ______________________

Is there a flavour you don't like? Which one?

____

What kinds of ice cream toppings do you like the best?

____

BREAKFAST

Which breakfast food do you like the most?

Cold cereal ___ Hot cereal ___

Pancakes ___ Paratha ___ Eggs ___

Orange Juice ___ Pineapple Juice ___Tomato Juice ___

GENERAL

Do you have any allergies? YES ___ NO ___

If YES, what? ______________________

Do you sleepwalk? YES ___ NO ___

Party Themes

Gwen wants her party to have a theme that will help her pick fun activities. Look at the ideas she's written. Then add some ideas of your own.

THEME #1: Flower Power

1. Plant flowers.
2. Decorate flower pots.
3. Make paper flowers.

THEME #2: Swap Shop

1. Collect outgrown clothing and other things I no longer use. Ask my friends to do the same.
2. Trade things so that we all get something new!

THEME #3: Let's Help

1. Find out about people and places in our neighbourhood that need help with something.
2. Make an action plan to do good in our town.

THEME #4: ______

1. ________________
2. ________________
3. ________________

Party Games

Gwen has made games for her friends to play at her party. You can play these games, too.

HOW TO PLAY:

1. Carefully pull out the picture posters on pages 10 to 14. Decide which game to play first—The Butterfly Game or Dress-Up Gwen.
2. Cut out the playing pieces on this page and on pages 15 and 16.
3. Have each player write her name on her playing piece.
4. Put a small piece of tape at the top of each playing piece so that players can tape their cutouts onto the big pictures.
5. Securely tape the big picture poster onto a wall or door.
6. Let each player take a turn.
7. When it's her turn, a player wears a blindfold so that she cannot see.
8. The other players spin her around and then point her in the direction of the big picture.
9. The player tapes her playing piece on the picture.
10. For The Butterfly Game, the player whose butterfly lands closest to the centre of the flower wins.
11. For the Dress-Up Gwen game, all players who put their pieces in the right places on the picture of Gwen are winners.

Cut out the butterflies. Use these pieces to play The Butterfly Game on pages 11 and 14.

Fun Facts about Butterflies:

- There are about 28,000 different kinds of butterflies.
- The smallest butterfly has a wingspan of about 1/2 cm.
- The largest has a wingspan of about 30 cm.
- A butterfly can fly at up to 19 km/h.
- The monarch butterfly has the longest migration route of any butterfly. It travels about 3,000 km from its northern summer home to its southern winter home each year.
- Butterflies can be found on every continent—except Antarctica.
- A person who studies butterflies is called a lepidopterist.

DRESS-UP GWEN

THE BUTTERFLY GAME

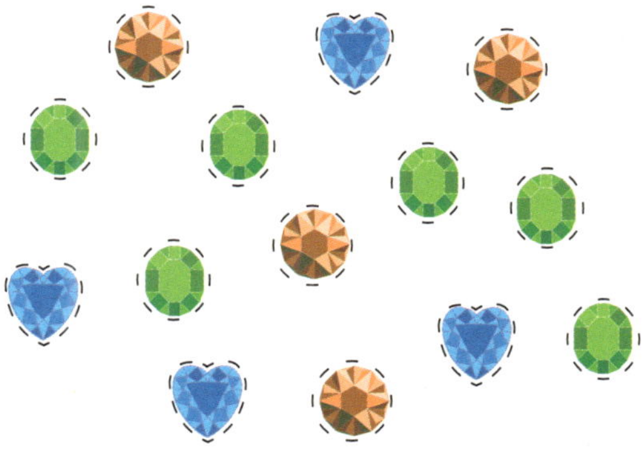

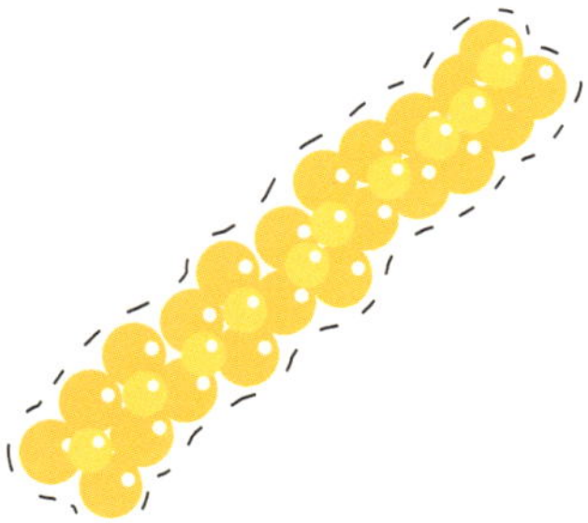

Thanks for coming to my party!

What do you want to play next?

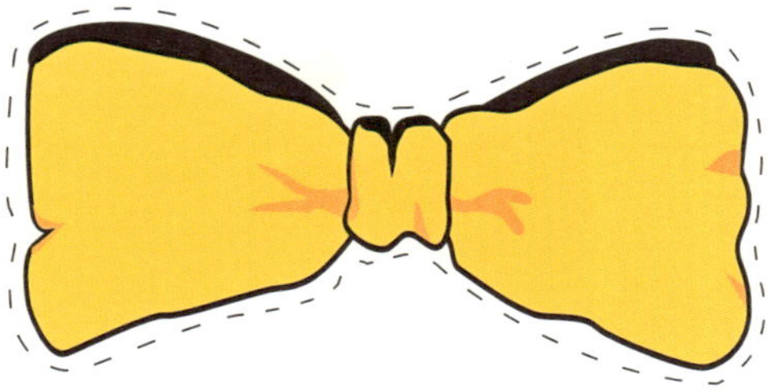

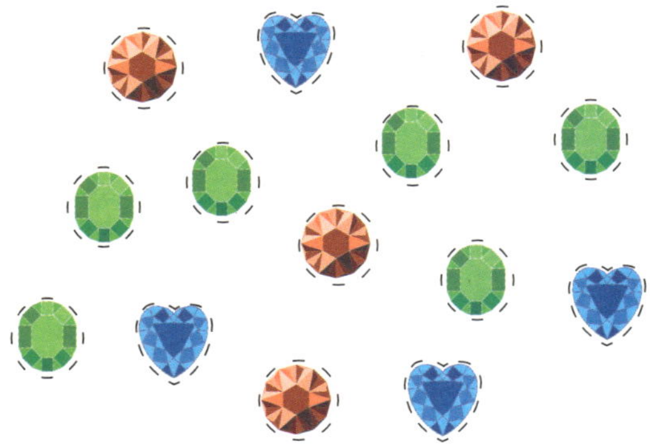

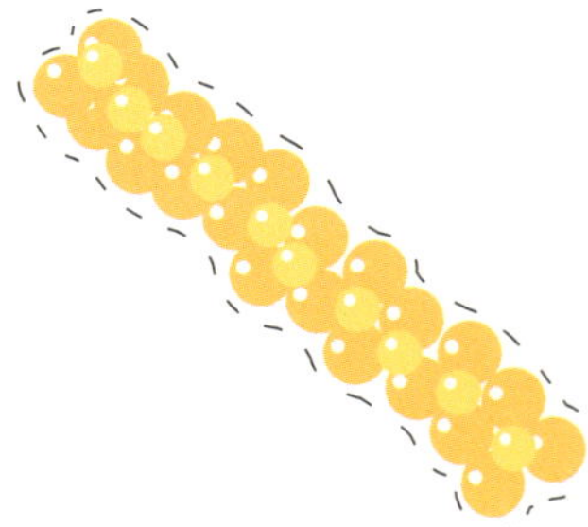

Thanks for coming to my party!

What do you want to play next?

More Party Games

Gwen and her friends played these games, too.
Would you and your friends like to play?

Game #1: The Alphabet Game

WHAT YOU NEED:

- a small, pretty box

WHAT YOU DO:

1. Players stand in a circle.
2. The first player holds the box and says, "I have an _____ in my surprise box." She fills in the blank by naming something that begins with the letter A.
3. She then passes the box to the player on her right. That player says, "I have a _______ in my surprise box." She names something that begins with B.
4. Players keep passing the box to the right, with each player naming something that begins with the next letter of the alphabet.
5. If a player can't name anything that begins with that letter, the player starts the alphabet over again with something that begins with A.
6. Keep playing until the group has named things all the way to the letter Z.

Game #2: Name That Book!

WHAT YOU NEED:

- small pieces of paper—one for each player
- a pen or pencil
- a timer that can mark one minute

WHAT YOU DO:

1. Each player writes the name of a book she likes on her piece of paper.
2. Every other player gets to ask one question about the book, such as "Is this book part of a series?" or "Is the main character of this book a boy or a girl?"
3. After all players have asked a question, the group has one minute to discuss the clues and to think of the title. The group gets three chances to guess.
4. If the group guesses correctly, each member gets one point.
5. If the group cannot guess, the player shows the name of the book to the group. Then she gets one point.
6. Keep playing until every player has had a chance to name her book.

Game #3: Musical Bear

WHAT YOU NEED:
- a teddy bear or other plush animal
- a music player

WHAT YOU DO:
1. One player is the music master. She controls when the music starts and stops. She sits with her back to the other players.
2. The other players sit in a circle, facing each other.
3. When the music starts, the players pass the teddy bear around the circle. When the music stops, the girl holding the bear drops out of the circle.
4. Keep playing until only one player is left.

Game #4: Ick!

This game is not for the squeamish! It's even more fun played in the dark with scary music in the background.

WHAT YOU NEED:
- a paper bag for each player or team
- two grapes or olives
- a small amount of cooked, cold noodles
- a slice of dampened bread
- five orange slices
- five pickles

WHAT YOU DO:
1. Have friends work alone, in pairs, or in groups of three, depending on how many players you have.
2. Place one of the items from the list above into each bag.
3. Pass each team a bag and have them reach their hands inside without looking. As they touch what's inside, tell them that you're about to explain what's inside each bag.
4. Tell a scary story, such as this one that Gwen told to Ben: An alien monster blew up. I collected the pieces in paper bags. One bag has the monster's eyeballs. One has its brains. One has its tongue. One has its fingers, and one has its toes. Who has each thing?
5. See who screams and drops the bag first!

Cut out and photocopy the placemat on the next page. →

______ 's Slumber Party Placemat

Play Tic-Tac-Toe

Make a Face!

Which one is different?

Complete the picture.

Jokes to Share

1. Why did the bacon laugh?
2. What vegetables are dangerous on boats?
3. Why don't strawberries like to drive?
4. What's the best way to make a milkshake?

Answers
1. Because the egg cracked a yolk!
2. Leeks
3. They're afraid of getting caught in a traffic jam.
4. Scare it.

Party Decorations

Gwen is making paper lanterns to decorate her room for her party. You can make a paper lantern, too.

WHAT YOU NEED:

- safety scissors
- stapler

WHAT YOU DO:

1. Cut out the template from pages 21 and 22.
2. Fold along the fold line.
3. Cut on the cut lines.
4. Unfold and make a long cylinder shape as shown.
5. Staple the two ends of the cylinder together.
6. Attach the handle, using two staples.

* Under adult supervision.

Party Favours

Gwen wants to give each of her guests a little gift to thank her for coming to the party. Here are some ideas she is considering. Which gift would you like to make? Which one would you like to get?

Special Sachet

WHAT YOU NEED:
- petals that have fallen from flowers (You can get them from a florist or from your garden.)
- gauzy fabric
- ribbon

WHAT YOU DO:
1. Place petals in the middle of a small square of fabric.
2. Fold the fabric and tie it with a pretty bow.

Music CD

WHAT YOU NEED:
- computer with Internet access or already imported music
- blank CDs

WHAT YOU DO:
1. Create a playlist of tunes that will remind your friends of your party.
2. Burn the playlist onto the CDs.
3. Give each guest her own copy of the party CD.

Perfect Pictures

WHAT YOU NEED:
- digital camera and photo printer
- cardboard to make frames
- glitter glue, crayons, and/or ribbons to decorate frames

WHAT YOU DO:
1. Take a portrait picture of each guest and make a print of each.
2. Decorate each frame—or let each friend decorate her own.
3. Tape each picture into a frame.

My Party

Gwen writes about all of her adventures and good times in her diary. After your party, you can write down your memories, too.

Dear Diary,

Let me tell you all about my party! My friends ______________, ______________, ______________, ______________, and ______________ helped me celebrate.

We played these games: ______________ ______________, ______________, and ______________. We had lots to eat, including ______________ and ______________.

One funny thing that happened was ______________ ______________ ______________ ______________.

For favours, I gave each guest a ______________ ______________. I hope they liked what I picked out.